First published 2009 by Walker Books Ltd
87 Vauxhall Walk, London SE11 5HJ

2 4 6 8 10 9 7 5 3 1

Text © 2009 Richard Platt
Illustrations © 2009 David Parkins

The right of Richard Platt and David Parkins to be identified
as author and illustrator of this work respectively has been asserted
by them in accordance with the Copyright, Designs and Patents Act 1988

Editor Lucy Ingrams
Designer Patrick Insole
Consultant Dr Philip de Souza, BA, MA, PhD

This book has been typeset in Truesdell and Herculanum

Printed in China

British Library Cataloguing in Publication Data:
a catalogue record for this book is available from the British Library

ISBN 978-1-84428-737-6

www.walker.co.uk

*My mistress
and Lydia*

*My master,
Gaius Martius*

Marcus and Lucullus

Apollo

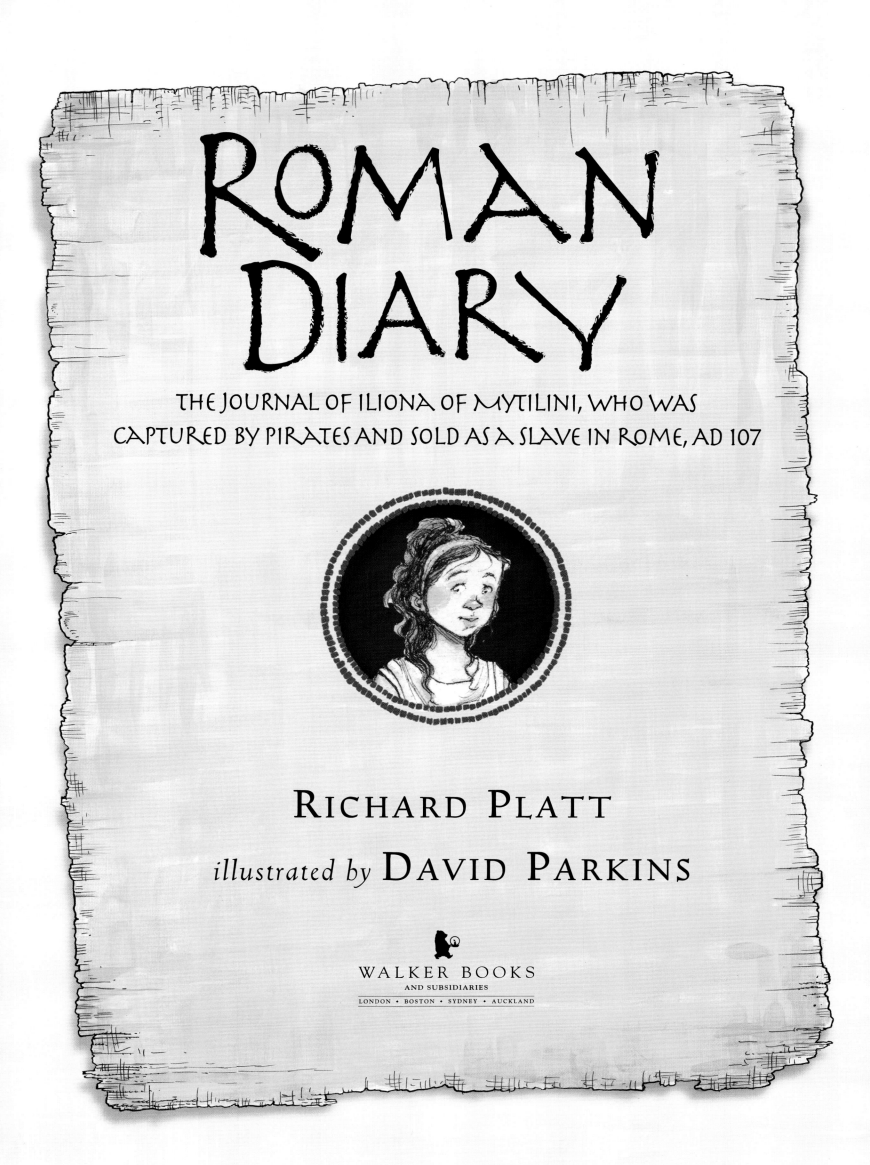

ROMAN DIARY

THE JOURNAL OF ILIONA OF MYTILINI, WHO WAS
CAPTURED BY PIRATES AND SOLD AS A SLAVE IN ROME, AD 107

Richard Platt

illustrated by David Parkins

WALKER BOOKS
AND SUBSIDIARIES
LONDON • BOSTON • SYDNEY • AUCKLAND

·CONTENTS·

NOTES FOR THE READER ON ILIONA'S WORLD

Cratinus

Cestius

Cytheris

Our doorman

The overseer

A New Diary For My New Life In Egypt, Year 3 Of The 221ST Olympiad.

My thoughts run faster than my pen as I write this, for today I learned that our lives are about to change – we are to sail to Egypt on a galley that leaves the day after tomorrow!

We must make this sudden journey because my father has learned that a warehouse he owns in Egypt has burned to the ground. He must travel there immediately to see it rebuilt. Mother, my brother Apollo and I will all travel with him, and make our home in Alexandria for two years at least.

It is a thrilling and wonderful idea, for I have never left our Greek island before. We have a fine, big house here on Mytilini, but in Egypt we will have an even bigger one. Everything else will be different, too. This, in truth, is why I have begun a diary, so that I might write down all that we do each day, and record everything new while it is still fresh.

To help in this project, my mother has given me a writing set – a bundle of fine goose-quills tied with a purple ribbon, a knife to sharpen them, a travelling ink-pot and a roll of the finest papyrus I have ever seen. Its surface is as smooth as the skin on Apollo's back.

In just two days, we shall board our ship in the harbour here, and set sail from Mytilini across the warm Aegean Sea. I think I shall like to stand at the front, let down my hair and feel the salt wind comb and curl it! In little more than a week we shall be in Alexandria. I cannot wait for this adventure to begin…

ILIONA

DISASTER·STRIKES·US!

FIRST DAY OF OUR VOYAGE

This morning before dawn we came aboard our ship. As the sun rose, the crew put out their oars and began to beat a splashing tune on the water. From land, I have often watched boats leaving the harbour: they seem to glide gracefully over the blue sea. From the deck, the view is different: a hundred men or more must strain every muscle to push the boat forwards.

This morning, though, the crew did not labour for long. The wind blew from the land, and once a sail was raised, they could rest. I stood at the front of the ship with Apollo to let the wind comb my hair, as I had dreamed. Instead it teased it into a knotted mass which took an hour to untangle!

❁❁❁

FIFTH DAY

Pity us! Apollo and I have lost everything we loved and cherished. Now we are orphans and slaves, to be bought and sold like goats.

We were but half a day from Rhodes when a sail appeared behind us. From the shape of the ship and the way it cut through the water, the crew could tell that it was a pirate craft. Our mariners rushed to their oars, but though they strained and pulled, the dark outline grew ever bigger behind us.

In the battle that followed, my mother drowned and my father was run through with a pirate sword. My tears flowed but I could do nothing. The pirates were not interested in the ship's cargo of wine, only in taking slaves, which they called "self-loading cargo". They took from Apollo and me all we possessed except my ink, pens and papyrus. These they let me keep because they guessed I will fetch a better price if it is obvious I know my letters.

Our journey to Egypt is at an end. Now we have begun another journey, to the very centre of the world: Rome.

❁❁❁

The pirates quickly sorted us out: the old, ill and crippled, they fed to the fishes.

The pirate ship's ram shattered the deck rail.

WE·ARE·SOLD

MY THIRD DAY IN ROME

We reached this strange and enormous city two days ago – not directly, but by hopping like frogs – for we were bought and sold three times on the way.

At each auction Apollo and I clung to each other, in case we should be sold apart, but – praise be to Zeus – it has not happened and other children have joined our miserable band. At each auction our price rises (though mine more than Apollo's, for I can speak fluent Latin and read a few words, but he struggles to write even in Greek). Finally we came into the port of Ostia on a stinking barge, which I think must have carried rotten fish before us.

We were herded quickly through the streets to some dark, cramped lodgings. We had food to eat – bread, oil and olives – but we were all filthy from our long journey. Creatures moved in my hair; my clothes were like rags and my eyes were red from crying.

Today two women came to the room in which we were locked with the other children. They took us out and gave us water and oil to wash. Then they cleaned our hair with fine toothed combs to remove the lice and gave us new garments to wear. I could not help but enjoy this, until one of my companions snapped, "Idiot! Can't you see that they prepare us for sale again?"

❁❁❁

During the journey to Rome, we travelled on foot (much) …

… by ship (also much) …

… in a cart (twice) …

… and on donkeys (once).

MY FOURTH DAY

The women returned this morning. They hung wooden signs round each of our necks. I was quite pleased that I could read the Latin words on mine: "Greek maiden". They also dusted our feet with chalk. This, I learned, was to show that we were newly taken as slaves, and so likely to be a troublesome buy.

"Greeks for sale!" the traders shouted as they pushed Apollo and I onto a little platform so that everyone in the crowd could see us clearly.

When the bidding began, it was brisk, and we were sold to a tall man who bought no other slaves in the sale. As he pressed through the crowd towards us, I was relieved that Apollo and I had been bought as a single lot – but, anxious about what would become of us, I asked the man where we were going. He cocked his head and raised his eyebrows, as if he couldn't have been more surprised to hear a dog speak Latin.

"You're the property of Gaius Martius," he replied. "He's a senator, and I'm his overseer. You'll work in his *domus* here in Rome." He turned Apollo's right hand over to look at the palm. "Judging by the smoothness of his hands," he said, "your brother has never done a stroke of work, but he'll be useful on my master's farm in the hills."

Then he pushed us forward into the square. "Come on. Shake that chalk off your feet!"

❀❀❀

The trader sang my praises, saying I could read and write. He said rather less about my brother.

I·SAY·FAREWELL·TO·APOLLO

THE SIXTH DAY

My parting from Apollo came sooner than I dreamed possible. For seeing me sob all the way from the auction, the overseer clearly decided he'd have no peace until we were separated.

When we reached the house, he pushed me into a little room close to the door, and bolted it. I hammered with my fists but simply got bruised and splintered. I lay on the bed and tried to forget I was a prisoner by writing everything that had happened that morning in this journal.

I must have slept afterwards, for when I awoke the door was open and a little lamp burned in an alcove in the wall, casting shadows across the room. When one of them moved, I sat up quickly.

"Don't be afraid," the shadow said, and I saw its owner, a girl a couple of years older than me. She told me she was a slave too, and that I would be happy here, for the master was a kind and generous man, "… and his wife doesn't whip us unless we deserve it!" she added. I asked her name, but before answering, she leaned out of the door and bellowed, "She is awake!"

She had just told me she was called Cytheris, when a tall and finely dressed woman swept into the room and shooed her out.

"Iliona – that is your name, isn't it?" the woman asked, turning to me. "I want you to know how welcome you are," she said, but didn't smile.

Apollo and I wept bitterly when the overseer separated us.

I asked if I could see Apollo. She looked puzzled, then left the room. A moment later, my little brother shuffled in.

I jumped up and threw my arms round his neck. We sat for a moment on the bed together, but before we had time to say much, the woman came back. In her arms was a sleeping child, about a year old.

The overseer followed her in, so I guessed what was to come. I screamed and begged him not to take Apollo, but it made no difference. He pushed us roughly apart.

Seeing my tears, the woman sat down, and put her arm around my shoulder. This started me sobbing again, and the child awoke. I thought she would cry too, but instead she grabbed my hand, and began sucking on my little finger.

More gently this time, her mother – my new mistress – began talking to me again. I was to be a companion and teacher for little Lydia, she said. I would also teach Greek to Lydia's half-brothers, Marcus and Lucullus. "We wanted to buy you because you already knew some Latin," she explained.

Her arm round my shoulder, the warmth of the room, the child in her arms – all these things reminded me of home and my own mother – not in a sad way but (to my surprise) in a way that comforted me. And for a moment I forgot my sorrow and began to wonder if I might be happy here.

❀❀❀

Apollo's hands were untied now, so he could hug me.

MY·STUDIES·BEGIN·AGAIN

DAY III OF THE MONTH OF MAIUS, YEAR 890

I had imagined that a slave's life here in Rome would be one of locks and chains. But there is nothing to keep me from running away.

Yet to where would I run, and why would I try? I am beginning to see that in Rome, slavery and freedom are not opposites, like night and day, or winter and summer. The poorest Roman citizens are worse off than many slaves. Here I have clothes (though it's true they are simple linen); my stomach never aches with hunger (though the food is plain) and I can rest when I am tired.

It would be simple to distract the doorman and slip into the street.

I sleep in a room with Cytheris, and in this I feel I am lucky. Cytheris keeps me company, and is teaching me much about Rome. Last night I learned about the calendar. Romans count the years from the date Rome itself was founded. The months are about thirty days long, and are each differently named. The days are more difficult, and for now I will just make my diary by counting up from the first day of each month.

DAY IV

This day I began my studies. It was also the first time I had set foot outside since the auction.

I had expected to study at home, as girls always do in Greece. But instead I went to school with Marcus and Lucullus. The three of us walked there, through the streets, with Cestius, the boys' *pedagogus*.

Cestius is an old slave, part-tutor, part-guardian.

The boys tormented a flea-bitten dog.

I was surprised at how humble the school is. On Mytilini, Apollo studied in a grand building with a hundred other boys. This one was just a tiny room with a few stools and an armchair for the teacher. Cestius made fun of my surprise: "This is one of the better ones!" he told me. "Most boys sit in the street to study."

Our class was not so different from my brother's school in Mytilini. Mostly we write on the same wax-coated tablets, though my *stylus* is shaped like the letter "T". With its flat end I can flatten the wax when I make mistakes, which I think is a fine idea, for I make many.

We studied reading and writing from early morning until noon, when Cestius came back. We walked home along Etruscan Street, which is lined with the most exotic kinds of shops.

In fact, my nose found the street before my eyes, because all the incense and perfume sellers have their stalls here.

The street is very busy, and Cestius took my hand. "Keep your eyes peeled," he told us, "for there are thieves around every corner here. They will skin you alive and sell you back your own hide before you even realize you've been robbed."

We saw no thieves, but we did have to flatten ourselves against the wall as a huge cart rumbled past, carrying building stone and timber. Our limbs seemed to be more at risk than our purses!

❁❁❁

The cart had solid wooden wheels and was pulled by a grumpy ox.

WE·VISIT·NERO'S·BATHS

DAY XVI OF MAIUS

Tomorrow we shall visit the baths. Though we have a bathroom here, with a small tub, Cytheris tells me we are going somewhere altogether more grand – the baths of Nero, who ruled Rome fifty years ago. A cruel man hated by all Romans, Cytheris says, his reputation earned him a saying: "What could be worse than Nero, or better than his baths?"

❁❁❁

DAY XVII

How can I begin to describe Nero's baths? They are more like a palace. The huge building towers above the neighbourhood; a gurgling "aqueduct" (a river on legs) brings water from the distant hills, and steam pours from the windows. The baths are so cheap they are almost free. Anyone who has a *quadrans* – Rome's smallest coin – can soak all afternoon.

It seemed that a visit to the baths was a chance for my mistress to show off how many slaves she can afford, for she insisted that every one of us come with her. We set off in the afternoon: two carried her in a litter, one walked ahead, and the rest of us followed.

Once we were inside and had changed into our *subligari* and *mamillares*, my mistress set one of us to guard our clothes, and took two more to wash, oil and massage her. The rest of us could do as we pleased for the afternoon.

Cytheris took me from room to room, until we came to the hot bath, the steamy *caldarium*. Here we lounged, pampering each other until we met some friends of Cytheris'. When she introduced me as newly enslaved, they were all very sorry for me.

As we talked, each revealed how they had become slaves. Most had been born of slave parents, but one blonde girl, from Germany, had been taken by Roman soldiers when they crushed a revolt there.

❁❁❁

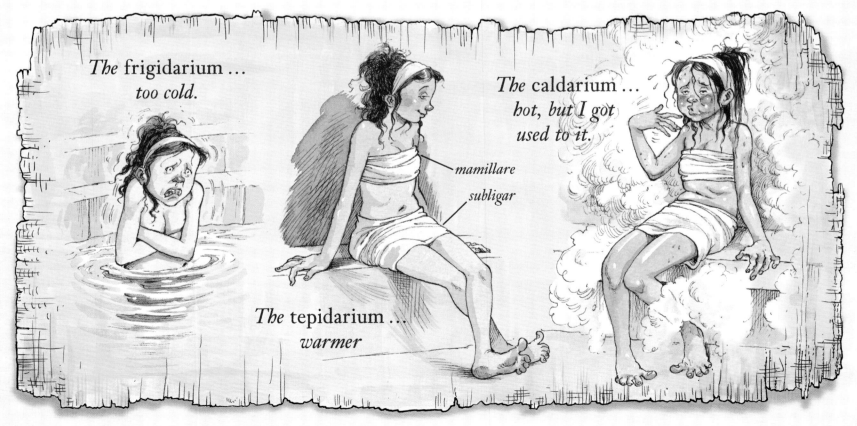

The frigidarium ... *too cold.*

The tepidarium ... *warmer*

mamillare
subligar

The caldarium ... *hot, but I got used to it.*

Cytheris showed me how to use a strigil to scrape my skin, and rubbed me with perfumed oil, which I guess she had drained from our mistress's bottle while her back was turned.

DAY XX

A fortnight ago I wrote a letter to Apollo, and gave it to my mistress. She promised that the overseer, who regularly travels between Rome and the farm, would take it to him, but I have had no reply.

❁❁❁

DAY XXV

This morning I awoke with a thundercloud around my head. I had dreamed that Apollo and I were back on Mytilini, doing the things we used to do together before we were captured – running on the open hills and swimming in the sea. When I awoke, the walls around me felt like a prison.

My master saw my long face, and I told him about my dream. He tried to make me feel better about living here in Rome, finishing with the words "there is always a chance of manumission". I didn't understand this Latin word, so he explained that good and obedient slaves may be freed through the kindness of their masters, or may buy their freedom with the money they earn.

His words lifted my stifling gloom and I began to hope that I might not live my whole life as a slave.

❁❁❁

It's the noise of the baths that you notice first: an echoing clamour as (it seems) half the population of Rome has come to bathe.

I·AM·SENT·ON·AN·ERRAND

DAY XXVII OF MAIUS

I learned today that the older brother of Marcus and Lucullus, is a legionnaire, who will be returning to Rome soon for the triumph of the Emperor Trajan. This grand parade is to celebrate the victory of Roman forces in Dacia, and it will be a fantastic spectacle which all of Rome will watch.

DAY XXIX

I made the mistake of talking to Cytheris about manumission. "Are you mad?" she exploded. "We earn a few *asses* pocket money a week for skivvying around this house. There are 16 *asses* in a *denarius*. They paid 500 *denarii* for you. It would take three lifetimes of work for you to buy your freedom." Then she threw a cushion at me and ran from the room in tears.

Now I am as full of sorrow as before – and guilty too, for having reminded her of how hopelessly trapped we both are.

"Do the arithmetic, Iliona!" Cytheris yelled.

"The dogs and bed-bugs left last night, and when they go, only a madman stays!" the seamstress said.

DAY I OF THE MONTH OF IUNIUS

My mistress sent me on an errand this morning. It was the first time I have ventured out into Rome's streets on my own. My task was to collect some embroidery from a seamstress who lived on the top floor of an apartment block.

Even by the standards of Rome (which are low), it was a crumbling wreck. The seamstress was hurrying to pack and practically threw the work at me. "The walls will come down, Greek girl," she warned me, "sure as Trajan's the emperor."

As I hurried down the stairs, I saw everyone else who dwelled or worked there leaving. One just jerked his thumb over his shoulder and said, "Hasten!" A huge crack had appeared in the side of the building! I did just that and breathed a sigh of relief when I was out in the street once more.

But my ordeal was not yet over. It was no great distance back to my home, but the streets lack signs and names, and finding your way is more like guesswork than navigation. In my haste, I took a wrong turn and in vain gazed about me for a shop, a house, a tree that I recognized. As I struggled, I heard a voice behind me.

"Are you lost?"

I spun round to face an elderly, white-haired man dressed in a clean and neatly-pressed *toga*. Such was my panic that I could not remember a word of Latin, and answered in Greek. "Yes! Where am I?"

To my amazement, he replied in Greek. "I am Greek too, though I have lived here most of my life. Where do you live?"

I told him my master's house was on the Quirinal hill, not far from Hill Gate, and close to where a huge fig tree grows. "I know the place," the old man said. He beckoned to me to follow and within a fourth part of an hour, he had led me home.

I turned around to thank my new-found friend but he was already ten paces away. "You are lucky. Gaius Martius is a good man," he shouted over his shoulder.

I was too far away to reply, so I just waved. I wonder if I will see him again to thank him properly for his help?

❀❀❀

I never expected to meet another Greek so soon.

DAY III

I learned that the apartments I visited collapsed just an hour after I was there. Cytheris didn't even seem surprised. "Two or three come down each week," she said.

❀❀❀

DAY V

The task of emptying the chamber pots is shared among all the slaves. Today it was my turn. I was about to empty them into the drain next to the kitchen, when Cytheris hissed, "Stop!"

She explained that urine is used here in Rome for cleaning clothes, and is bought and sold, and even taxed!

I found this hard to believe, but that night a stinking wagon drew up and the driver tipped the foul liquid into a jar.

For this (Cytheris told me), we receive a few *quadrantes* each week. I have decided that I shall save mine to buy Apollo's freedom.

❀❀❀

I·MEET·A·SOLDIER

DAY VII OF IUNIUS

We were woken last night by a tremendous tumult. My master's eldest son, Cratinus, had returned. He had tried to slip in through the back door without attracting attention, but instead awoke the doorman, who took him for an intruder, and challenged him. By the time the misunderstanding had been untangled, the whole house was awake and gathered in the *peristylum*.

Cratinus seemed to me very haughty and pleased with himself, and I was soon bored with the spectacle, and slipped back to bed.

❀❀❀

DAY VIII

Cratinus is just like the soldiers who guard the fort on Mytilini: they think armour and scars make it impossible for girls to resist their charms. I had to endure an hour of his stories about how brave he had been in Dacia. It was dull in the extreme, though he did make me laugh once or twice.

❀❀❀

DAY X

I foolishly smiled at Cratinus this morning when I was in the kitchen preparing food for baby Lydia. Taking this as encouragement, he pinched my bottom. I spun round and spat out my fury at him, ending with, "And if you pinch me again, I shall tell your parents!"

At this, he threw back his head and laughed. "Tell them. Tell anyone you like. Tell all of Rome. For you are just a slave girl, and I can do whatever I like."

I think he would have gone further if I had not been holding a kitchen knife. But he just picked up a fig, pushed it whole into his fat mouth, and walked out into the *atrium*.

❀❀❀

DAY XI

Cratinus has injured his foot. He was showing off to his brothers in the *peristylum*, pretending to assault a statue, when his sword glanced off its marble arm, and nearly took off one of his toes. Now he worries that he will not be able to march in Emperor Trajan's triumph in six days' time. I shall be glad if he cannot.

❀❀❀

A burglar the size of Cratinus could not really be stopped by our elderly doorman.

DAY XIII

At dinner today, I brought in a dish just as the family were teasing Cratinus about his endless war stories.

Suddenly he lost his temper. "Do you want to know what Dacia was really like?" he yelled. Without waiting for a reply, he continued, "Shall I tell you how Decebalus set fire to everything as he retreated, so that we had nothing to eat as we followed him?

"Or perhaps you'd like to know about the Battle of Tapae? Oh yes, our emperor's great victory, but it wasn't quite as glorious as you may have heard. The grass was red with Roman blood, and there were so many injured that the emperor tore his cloak into strips to make bandages."

For a moment, it was so quiet that I could hear the fountain outside in the *atrium*, then our master said quietly, "Cratinus: we know how much you have suffered, but there are children here. Why don't you go and rest?"

Cratinus got up and slowly left the room.

After that, I felt a little sorry for Cratinus. All the same I was relieved to learn from Cytheris that he will not be with us for much longer. His legion will leave Rome directly after the triumph.

Cratinus' smile, which has never left his face since he arrived, had vanished.

Soldiers struck victorious poses on the huge floats.

WE·WATCH·THE·TRIUMPH!

Our complete household was in a state of great excitement at the thought of watching today's triumph. All except for Cytheris, who had to stay behind to look after little Lydia. We had been fighting for a week over which of us would go. In the end Cestius tossed dice and I won, which threw Cytheris into a great sulk.

It was still dark when we left the house, but the streets were turned almost as bright as day by the torches of the people who had flocked to see the spectacle. They so crowded the street that my master and mistress were forced to abandon their sedan chairs, and walk like common people. They shuffled slowly to Octavian's Walks, where the senators and other dignitaries were to greet the emperor. I went with Marcus, Lucullus, Cestius and the other seven slaves to find a place to stand.

We seemed to wait for ever before there was anything to look at. While we hopped impatiently from foot to foot, I spotted some distance away the white-haired Greek who had helped me home. I yelled and waved, but he did not hear me. Then a terrific roar from the crowd told us the parade had begun, and a moment later soldiers in brilliant, shiny armour filled the road to bursting point.

I looked for Cratinus, thinking I would spot him from his limp, but all the troops marched in perfect time. Then I saw the emperor himself, in a magnificent golden chariot, drawn by four white horses. A slave held a laurel wreath above his head. He wore no helmet and I realized for the first time, he was just a man like any other.

When I told Cestius I thought I had expected to see a god, he snorted. "All emperors think they're gods."

When Trajan and more of his troops had passed, I picked up my cloak. But Marcus hissed, "Not YET! WATCH!" Turning back, I thought I was seeing something magical. For round the corner came an entire building, several storeys in height. A hundred bearers carried it on their shoulders, moving at a brisk walk. Another of these great floats followed, then many more, so that the procession continued for another hour.

Following behind was a sad sight: thousands of chained prisoners taken captive in the war with the Dacians walked behind their leaders. These men all knew they were living their last minutes.

The crowd now began to press towards the Forum to see the fate that awaits those who oppose the mighty Roman Empire. But I had no taste for this, and even the boys looked pale.

We hurried home as well as we could.

Centurions led the defeated leaders to the Forum.

I·VISIT·THE·SENATE

DAY XX OF IUNIUS

I am soon to see my brother again! As I sat with Lydia this afternoon, Cytheris came and told me that in one month we shall be travelling to my master's estate in the Sabine Hills. We shall stay there through the hottest weeks of the summer – and I shall have the chance to spend some time with Apollo, if his work allows. I am glad, for he has not replied to any of the letters I sent him.

❁❁❁

DAY XXII

This day our master went to sit in the Senate, which always causes much upheaval. He dreads going, but loves it when he gets there. Making Rome's laws makes him feel important, and he sees all his friends. Most are very old, and I suspect that they take secret bets on which of them will die first.

It was halfway through the morning when my mistress let out a shriek. "Hell's teeth, he's left his medicine behind!" I looked round, and sure enough, in a niche by the door was my master's flask of sea-grape wine. "Iliona, take it to him, or truly he will cough his lungs up."

I dashed to the Forum, and rushed through the door of the Senate House without stopping. Too late, I realized that the passageway led straight into the Senate chamber. I found myself surrounded by Rome's greatest, richest men.

❁ The room fell silent.

"Young lady," a senator finally addressed me, "I assume that your dramatic appearance is of the utmost importance, since the very future of Rome hangs upon the debate it interrupted."

Scanning the rows of seats, I spotted my master and held up the flask. "Senator Martius, you forgot your sea-grape wine."

There was another unbearable silence. Then I heard a stifled snigger from a younger senator at the back. One of his neighbours guffawed, and at length laughter echoed round the chamber. When it died down, someone shouted, "Take your potion, Gaius, your coughing has been been driving us all mad!"

As the laughter started again, a hand pulled the vial from my grip, and it was passed back to my master.

I didn't wait to see him drink, but fled the chamber as quickly as I had entered it.

❁❁❁

My master wears a purple-edged toga to the Senate and special red shoes with a crescent stitched to the front.

I wished that an earthquake would bring the marble columns and high roof down upon my head!

OUR·WATER·DRIES·UP

DAY I OF THE MONTH OF IULIUS, YEAR 860

This morning there was silence from the kitchen, which normally rings with the sound of water flowing endlessly from a pipe on the wall into a stone basin below.

"The aqueduct has burst once more!" my mistress exclaimed when she came down.

In my home, water always comes from a well, never from a spout in the wall. So she explained that our water here comes from springs four days' journey away. "It's beautiful, clear water, but to flow here, it crosses deep valleys on high, arched bridges. In other places it flows underground, through tunnels. Because of its length – more than 60,000 paces – the channel is always leaking."

In my first week in Rome, I had marvelled at the luxury of having water running in the house, but soon took it for granted. Now I appreciate it once more, for I have to pick up an *amphora* and join a long line of slaves at the fountain in the street outside.

The slaves from the houses nearby have a rare chance to talk together at the fountain.

DAY II

Little Lydia said her first Greek word today! It was "*Mamme*" – Mum in Greek. I cannot tell my mistress. She would be furious if she knew I spoke Greek to the baby and madder still if she knew Lydia thought I was her mother!

❀❀❀

DAY V

We still have no water in the house and today an errand took me past the aqueduct. From a gap in its side spills a torrent of water that rushes down onto the roofs of the houses below. On the bridge I saw stonemasons at work trying to block the hole with bags full of sand. Quite a crowd had gathered to watch, and I listened as a man shouted angrily at the supervisor of the water repairs. Judging from his fine, new *toga*, he was very wealthy.

"Why do the street fountains still flow when the water in my house has dried up?" the rich man demanded. "Beggars may drink, while my fountain is silent!"

The supervisor of the water repairs let out a deep sigh, before replying with exaggerated respect. "Because, sir, inside the *castellum* there is a barrier. Normally there is enough water to flow over it and into the pipes that lead into your fine abode –" here he made a little bow – "however, if the aqueduct bursts or leaks, the level falls. Then your pipes are cut off, but water continues to flow to the public fountains. In this way –" he paused, before delivering his crushing last line – "the poorest

The rich man's smart sandals got soaked, as he listened to the explanation.

citizens in Rome do not have the free water taken from them by those who can afford a supply to their own homes."

This bold response brought a round of applause, for we all expected the official would grovel to such a wealthy, important man.

Sniffing defeat, he edged away, muttering, "Ah yes, I see … um, thank you for that clear explanation," as he tried to hide his embarrassment.

❀❀❀

I returned past Cloaca Maxima, *the city's biggest sewer, which stank in the summer heat.*

WE·SET·OFF·FOR·THE·FARM

DAY XX OF IULIUS

We were supposed to leave for the country today, but during a thunderstorm last night, lightning bolts flashed in the direction of the Sabine Hills and everyone (but me) feared it was a sign that we should not travel.

To check whether it was truly a bad omen my mistress went to the temple of Jupiter Tonans, a thunder god, taking with her an offering of a chicken. (Cytheris says she cannot think the omen too serious, or she would have taken a pig at least.) She came back saying that it is safe to travel, so we depart tomorrow.

❀❀❀

DAY XXI

On this day I was woken by the snorts and braying of the donkeys, and the iron-ringed wheels of the two *raedae* they were pulling. We were to make an early start as builders' carts are the only wagons allowed into the crowded streets during the day.

"Get a move on!" the driver was grumbling when I went outside. "I'll be fined if we're not through Hill Gate by dawn."

I helped the others load the carriages with everything we would need on our journey. (Fortunately we had little luggage: most of it had left on a train of mules yesterday.) Then we flung ourselves inside.

And so we set off, driving along High Lane in complete darkness, guided by torches on the front-most carriage.

By the time the sun rose, we had left the walls of Rome behind us and were travelling through fields of waving flowers. These made me long for Mytilini, for in spring the hills there are a mass of different colours. These flowers, though, were in rows and all alike, and Cestius tells me they are grown for the vases of the city. In other fields lettuce and vegetables grew, and huge flocks of chickens scratched in the dust.

The heat, the early start, the rocking of the carriage, and the unchanging view (for the road was dead straight) all competed to see which could make me drowsy first.

To see if it was a good time for our journey, a priest sacrificed the bird, opened it and studied its guts.

Cytheris told me the postman might travel 100 miles in a day – three times as far as our creaking raeda *would carry us.*

cast puddles of light on a few patches of white wall and overhanging olive trees. Everything else disappeared into inky darkness.

Before we left Rome, I had dreamed that I would rush around the farm until I found Apollo, but I was so exhausted that I simply collapsed onto my bed and fell instantly asleep.

❀❀❀

My head flopped, and I jerked it upright a dozen times before finlly falling fast asleep. A loud shout woke me, and Cytheris grabbed my arm. I had slumped sideways and was about to fall out of the carriage tailgate.

I was shaking like a reed in a gale when she pulled me back inside. The road is surfaced with square stones so that it may resist the heaviest wagons without breaking up. Worse, the shout had come from a postman riding his horse at a gallop. Between the hard road and his horse's hoofs, my head would have been well and truly broken had I fallen.

When at last we arrived at the farm, it was dark once more. Marcus and Lucullus leaped down at the end of the drive, and raced ahead of us to the door, which was lit by torches. More of these

My master's villa in the Sabine Hills is very grand!

I·FIND·MY·BROTHER!

DAY XXII OF THE MONTH OF IULIUS

From the moment I awoke this morning, I could only think of finding Apollo. Yet this was the very thing I could not do. For the villa is a very different place from our house in Rome. There, my master and mistress lead busy lives and hardly notice if one of us is missing. Here, they are idle, with nothing better to do than to count us and ask, "Where's Cytheris?" or, "I haven't seen Iliona for some time. Where's she gone?"

So instead of searching for my brother, I had to be content with glancing from the windows to see if I could spot him. When I finally plucked up the courage to ask whether I could see Apollo, my mistress said curtly, "Perhaps tomorrow," and sent me to put the baby to bed.

Here Cytheris and I have separate rooms. We all retired early to bed this evening which has given my plenty of time to write in this diary.

❀❀❀

DAY XXV

I have finally met Apollo! Having seen me sulking and kicking my heels about my tasks, my master asked me what the matter was, and I said I longed to see my brother.

"Then you shall!" he said, and sent a message that the bailiff, who runs the farm, should fetch him.

32

*I hardly recognized Apollo –
his hair was matted and greasy,
and he stank like a goat.*

When the bailiff finally arrived with a boy, I stared and blinked. Was this Apollo? Only when he spoke my name was I sure, and I ran and threw my arms around him. Then I stood back and gazed at him. He was quite changed. He wasn't just thinner, he had bruises on his arms, and a red scar around one ankle. Worse, perhaps, were his eyes. They darted left and right, and he had the expression that I once saw on the face of a stag as it fled from the hunt.

I asked him if he was all right, and before answering Apollo turned to the bailiff. Only when the man nodded did he reply – and then in stuttering Latin. "I'm fine," he said. "They treat us well here, the work is not too hard and we get enough to eat…"

All this came without expression, like the worst actors I had seen in the theatre on Mytilini. Then he said in Greek, "I've missed you, but I cannot stay long. We are weeding the vines, and if I don't return my friends will have to do my row as well as their own. Goodbye."

He kissed me, and was gone.

❀❀❀

DAY XXVI

I have made friends with the house dogs. They are huge and black – whereas the herders' dogs are all white. I was curious about this, and asked the bailiff, who told me, "Why, think about it, girl. A guard dog must be black so that thieves who come in the night cannot see him. A herder's dog is best white so that he is not mistaken for a wolf."

❀❀❀

*The house dogs scared
me at first.*

SECRETS·OF·THE·FARM

DAY XXVII OF IULIUS

Last night I was woken by the small noise of something dry and hard falling on the floor of my room.

Outside, I heard the slap of bare feet running from my window. I crawled around to try and find whatever had been thrown in, but it was too dark. In the morning I found a short piece of bone. One side was scratched in a pattern. I took it to the window, and in the sunlight, I realized I was holding it upside down.

There, in tiny Greek letters, was a message: COME OUR HUTS IN 2 NIGHTS.

I didn't know how Apollo found out which my room was. Nor did I think I could wait that long to see him again, but I had no choice. So I continued with my tasks as if I was still in Rome.

Here, though, time seems to crawl past for, in fact, there is little for us to do. This morning, my mistress decided that she would like to take a walk with the baby while Cestius was teaching the boys. What this really meant was that she walked, while I carried Lydia.

From the road we could look down at row upon row of vines stretching down into the valley – and up, to the steeper slopes lined with olive trees. My mistress's conversation was mostly about how difficult it was to make money from a vineyard. I paid little attention until I heard her saying, "And that's where the labourers live."

My mistress pointed down the hill to a row of low shacks.

Apollo lifted his
shirt to show me
his flat stomach.
"I am often
hungry,"
he said.

DAY XXIX

Zeus must have been smiling on me last night, for there was a full moon. Once everyone was in bed, I had no difficulty slipping out of the window, and running down the drive through the moon shadows of the olive trees. Now I have learned the truth about Apollo's life on the farm.

"Iliona, I can't begin to describe how awful it is here," he told me. "We are prisoners. We mostly live on coarse bread and olives, and work eight days in every nine from dawn until dusk."

I asked him what happened to his ankle.

"One of us tried to escape. They picked him up, whipped him, shaved his head and branded his leg with an "F" for *fugitivus* – a runaway."

"But your ankle?"

"I'm coming to that. The overseer said we must all have known about the escape, so for a month we worked in chains. Then Gaius Martius arrived without warning one day, and saw what we endured. He sacked the overseer, putting an old slave in his place. Now things are not as bad as they were – we have new clothes, and time to rest in the hottest hours."

A dog began to bark and I was glad I had made friends with them. Apollo poked his head out of the hut. "You had better go. Don't try to come here again. It will be trouble for both of us." He pushed me out, and I sprinted back to the villa.

Only this morning did I realize how close I could have come to discovery. For the daylight revealed my dusty footprints, leading from the drive to my window!

35

FIRE!

DAY XV OF THE MONTH OF AUGUSTUS

Our stay in the hills finished yesterday, and we are back in Rome. I did not see Apollo again, apart from when we came just close enough to wave. My mistress frowned a silent warning when I asked if we could talk.

We had one exciting moment when rumours spread of slaves deserting a nearby farm. The shutters went up and the dogs were released in case we should all have our throats cut in the night by the *fugitivi*. In the end, though, it turned out to be false gossip.

❊❊❊

DAY XX

Yesterday I nearly lost my life – and became a heroine (though I am not sure I deserve the glory heaped on my shoulders)!

The day began normally enough: we set out for Agrippa's baths (not as nice as Nero's, for the water is less clear). We did not linger as long as usual, but instead went to the house of my mistress's friend nearby. Lydia was sleeping, and I took her crib to the other end of the house.

Not long after, there was a smell of smoke. Nobody was concerned for there is always smoke in Rome from people lighting cooking or heating fires with small wood, to set the charcoal alight. But the conversation turned to fires, such as the great fire fifty years ago that destroyed most of Rome.

Even when we heard cries in the street, there was no alarm. Our hostess looked out, but returned saying, "The fire is distant, and the wind blows it away from here."

But then came a loud hammering at the door. A boy hardly older than me, his face black with soot, asked for buckets, adding, "Have a care, the flames attack your walls!" At this exact moment, a billow of smoke blew into the room, as if Adranos the fire god himself had heard him.

Everyone rushed towards the *peristylum*. As soon as we got outside, we heard loud crackling, and felt heat on our faces. Hungry flames licked towards the room where the child slept and nobody did anything. While my mistress sobbed, all the other women wrung their hands. One muttered, "At least it isn't a male child."

Their stupidity made me furious and foolhardy. I plunged into the pool in the middle of the *peristylum* to soak my clothes, and covered my face with my wet scarf. Then I dashed towards the open door.

For the rest of my story, I rely on others, for all I remember is waking up in bed at home and immediately retching a foul black paste on to the bedclothes. When the room ceased to spin around me, I saw Cytheris who whispered, "I fetched our master from the Senate," and pointed to where he stood with my mistress at the end of the bed. They beamed, and my mistress said quietly, "You did a brave and fine thing, Iliona. We shall not forget this."

❊❊❊

It seems that I stumbled from the smoke and flames, dropped the crib and its squealing passenger, and fainted.

I·LIVE·AT·THE·WORLD'S·CENTRE

DAY XXV OF AUGUSTUS

Today my mistress received a letter from her brother, a legionary commander stationed on the outer edges of the empire. He is on a big cold island called Britannia, somewhere far to the north. It is farther even than Dacia, where Cratinus fought. And he does not like it.

The letter started an argument between my master and mistress. When she took her brother's part – that Britannia is cold and the people ignorant and not worth ruling – my master shrugged. "You forget, my dear, that Rome grows strong by conquest.

From these new provinces we get slaves and treasure. It's true that Britannia is, so far, a disappointment, but from Dacia, Trajan brought back half a million pounds of gold and double the weight of silver. And if the emperor had not defeated the Dacians, they would grow bolder. Soon they would be attacking Rome itself."

❁❁❁

DAY XXVII

On the way to school I asked Cestius about Rome's provinces, and before our class started, he pointed to a map pinned on the wall. "Look, here is the known world – Rome rules the part coloured red. How much is left?" I had to admit that most of the map was red.

When Cestius returned, he led us a different way home, through the Forum. When we reached a food stall, he pointed to everything on sale, saying, "Look: the grain comes from Egypt, the oil from Spain, the salt pork from Gaul – all Roman provinces." Next door, at a hide and fabric shop, the same… "Here is Egyptian linen, African cotton, leather from Britannia and furs from Asia Minor."

Then he stepped into the street and ran his hand over the shiny

My mistress's brother says that in Britannia sometimes the troops are so cold, they beat their legs with stinging nettles to keep warm.

stone pillar. "The marble that made this pillar came from your country, Iliona. So you see, almost everything we have in Rome comes from distant regions that our great city rules."

❀❀❀

DAY XXX

Though my mistress always looks well, I had no idea until today quite how much effort is needed to achieve this.

She called me in to her room after waiting an hour for Psecas, her *ornatrix* who comes to the house each day to do her hair. She was staring into a bronze mirror and applying the finishing touches to her face. She was wearing only an undershirt and called out, "Pass me that clean tunic, Iliona." without taking her eyes away from the mirror. Lying across the bed was a plain white tunic made of the finest silk I have ever seen. I couldn't resist running my hands through the fabric as I handed it to her.

However it wasn't her clothing that took the time, but her hair. At first she was patient, but when my work collapsed in a clumsy heap around her shoulders, she flew into a rage, shouting words I have only heard women in the market place use.

But at last she calmed down and between us, we made of her hair something that approached its normal appearance. As I left, she gave me four shiny *denarii* saying, "We shall make an *ornatrix* of you yet, and I can sack that lazy slug Psecas."

I have put the coins with the others I have been saving to free Apollo, under the loose tile on the floor.

❀❀❀

When I had combed her hair out …

I had to primp and pin it …

into a neat pile on the top of her head.

WE·WATCH·A·DEADLY·GAME

DAY 11 OF THE MONTH OF SEPTEMBER

I do not know how I should write about what I have seen today. We went to the *munera* – the "games" – at the amphitheatre. Except they are not like games I have ever played. They are real battles between two slaves, called gladiators, who fight with razor-sharp weapons. Today's games were the gift of the emperor to the people, as part of the celebration of the Dacian tiumph.

The gladiators fight in a big, open oval of sand in the middle. All around rise thousands of seats. To sit in one you must have a wooden token. My mistress gave one each to Cytheris and me as a treat. "Come and sit with me. We'll be right at the top!"

She wasn't joking. Women and slaves sit on the highest tier and low seats are reserved for the most important Romans, with senators – such as my master – at the very front. At first I was disappointed to be so far away, but when the spectacle began, I was glad. We could not smell the blood, nor see the fear on the faces of the defeated gladiators.

The first match was between a net-man and a pursuer. Though the pursuer fought bravely, he soon grew exhausted. When at last he stumbled, the net-man stood with his trident touching the pursuer's chest, and turned to the emperor's box for a signal.

I watched this hoplomachus defeat his foe with a well-timed blow from his heavy shield.

The Thracian's shield was so small, he really needed his leg armour.

The net-man seemed almost defenceless without a helmet or a sword.

The pursuer's helmet had a rounded crest to stop it snagging in the net.

*The trainer told us the animals will
only fight if they are driven by flaming torches.*

I looked away, but my mistress pulled at my arm, saying, "Iliona, don't worry. The pursuer fought well. The emperor will listen to the crowd." Looking up I saw the emperor spare the defeated man, and reward the winner with a wooden sword that meant he had won his freedom.

During the next fight, I watched everything. And by the third, I was actually enjoying it. The roar of the crowd ringing in my ears swept me along, as a strong wind blows down the road. But when the show ended, I felt ashamed.

As we queued to get out, we met my master who had a surprise for us. He led us away from the crowd and down into a basement below the arena. Here we saw ferocious lions, tigers and leopards pacing in their cages. They will fight in the ring tomorrow afternoon.

The trainer of beasts told us the animals are usually terrified of the gladiators who challenge them. So despite the excitement of the spectacle, I went home with a sad heart.

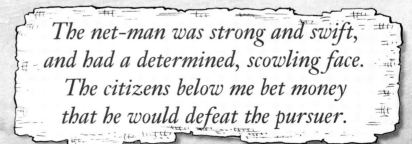

*The net-man was strong and swift,
and had a determined, scowling face.
The citizens below me bet money
that he would defeat the pursuer.*

Thousands of men swarmed all over the building, just like maggots on a dead dog.

I·AM·HOISTED·INTO·THE·SKY

DAY X OF THE MONTH OF SEPTEMBER

Today we accompanied my master on a visit to the site of some new baths. People say they will be finer than Nero's – and the biggest that Rome has ever seen. My master is one of the senators who encouraged the emperor to build these baths, in spite of the great cost of their construction.

We left at an early hour, before the sun got too hot. Several of the house slaves carried my master and mistress in chairs. Cytheris and I followed behind, talking. The baths stand just up the hill from the amphitheatre and it is easy to see them from wherever you are in the city.

As we arrived an important-looking man asked me in Greek, "Would you like to climb to the top?" He must have heard my accent. Of course I replied "Yes!" in Greek and he called over a mason who led me to a huge basket.

As soon as I stepped into it, the mason jumped in after me and waved his arm. At this signal two men began to walk inside a great wheel high above, setting it turning. To my great alarm, this made the basket rise into the air.

Higher and higher it climbed, until I could see every part of the baths. And I was astonished to learn that the walls are but a TRICK! From the outside, they look like solid marble. But in fact they are not at all.

The mason showed me how the builders mix lime with water and a kind of dust called *pozzolana*, so that it turns into a dark grey mess which they pour between moulds made of wooden planks. Within days, the mess turns hard, so that it stands up on its own, without the wooden moulds. Then the mason covers it in thin slabs of stone, though they look like solid blocks.

When I got back down to the steady ground, I could not find the Greek man to thank. On the way home, my mistress told me he is not Greek at all, but Syrian. "That was only Apollodorus, the Emperor's architect!"

❀❀❀

The mason beckoned to me to step out onto a giddy, windy platform at the very top of the building.

A·WICKED·TRIP

DAY XV OF THE MONTH OF SEPTEMBER

Cytheris is very proud. She has made friends with a stagehand at the theatre of Pompey, who will let us in to a performance there tomorrow afternoon. Our mistress will not learn of it, for she plans a visit to the temple at the same time, and does not want anyone to come with her.

❦❦❦

DAY XVI

Pompey's theatre is near Nero's baths, on the low ground by the big bend in the river. Inside, there is enough room for an audience of 20, 000 to sit down. Not that they ever do! In all the time we were there, hardly anyone stayed in their seats. They stood up to applaud and cheer – or to shout and heckle the actors. They walked back and forth too. Just as we arrived, half the audience left to watch a tightrope-walker in another part of the city.

The performance was unlike anything I have ever seen before. Cytheris called it a "pantomime". The star of this show stood at the centre of the stage, chanting and speaking at the top of his voice. Meanwhile, slaves made music with rattles, cymbals, drums and gongs.

The rest of the cast acted out the story in silence. The sweeping movements they made with their arms meant that those in the farthest seats could understand the action – even if they spoke only a little Latin.

I did not like the story! The chanting star told how a woman cheated her

husband. When some of the women in the cast took off their clothes I covered my eyes – though most of the audience roared with laughter. When one of the actors spotted us and practically lifted us from our seats, telling us, "This is no place for girls as young as you!", I was relieved that I didn't have to watch any more.

The most extraordinary sight completed our wicked trip. As we were marched to the exit Cytheris hissed, "Look, LOOK!"

I followed her eyes and saw our mistress sitting with some women friends in the seats above us, and she was laughing as loud as any of them. I put my finger to my lips, and we hurried home.

❦❦❦

Cytheris shouted, "We've got tickets!" (which of course we hadn't), but I was embarrassed.

46

The theatre is a huge building – bigger even than our theatre on Mytilini, which is the biggest in Greece.

I · WATCH · A · BANQUET

DAY XX OF THE MONTH OF SEPTEMBER

Today my mistress announced that she is to hold a banquet in honour of two newly appointed senators. "Nothing too grand," she added, "just nine of us." However, I have heard much of Roman banquets, and our cook was terrified at the thought of all the work, and ran around moaning, "How will we manage in our tiny kitchen?" He was calmed only when my mistress assured him that a caterer will prepare most of the food, and we will only reheat it here.

❀❀❀

DAY XXIII

I cannot quite believe the quantity of stuff that fills the kitchen and another room besides.

Some of it I do not even recognize. The butcher brought some beasts like rats, skinned and sewn up along the belly. I asked him what they were and he cheerfully replied, "Them's stuffed dormice, young lady. You cook them on a spit." I felt quite sick.

❀❀❀

"Them's delicious apparently, but I've never tasted them – couldn't afford them," the butcher told me.

DAY XXIV

My task tonight is to to stand at the side of the room with a jug of perfumed water and a towel, and before guests lie down to eat I shall wash and dry their hands and feet. I shall wash their hands between courses, too, if they command me to do so. This seems deadly dull, but I shall at least have the chance to listen to the conversation.

❀❀❀

Preparations began with the delivery of a small mountain of charcoal.

DAY XXVIII

I am so exhausted I can hardly write, though the feast finished more than a day ago. The guests began to arrive as the sun was setting, and were still here when it rose.

I have never seen such food! First, there was shellfish: mountains of oysters, mussels and spiny sea-hedgehogs. Then tiny songbirds huddled together on a golden platter. The stuffed dormice I had seen earlier, arrived dipped in honey and rolled in tiny black seeds. The main courses were kid, sucking pig and sow's udder – all stuffed and roasted.

There were entertainers too – dancing girls who tumbled and leaped in the air, musicians from Africa, a dwarf who ate fire, and a hunchback who told jokes about everyone there.

Of course there was wine: warmed wine, wine chilled with snow from the mountain tops, wine sweetened with honey, wine flavoured with costly spices. And then yet more wine, mixed with water just as people normally drink it.

Indeed, it was too much wine that ended the evening. One of the guests started talking about the new baths. He did not know how attached my master is to the project and began to rave about how "its great cost will destroy the empire."

When he finished, my master turned purple with rage. Nobody else dared speak. Moments later he left for his room, trembling like a leaf.

The bitter row shook everyone, and I felt exhausted by it (and by standing on my feet all night). When I got to bed, I fell instantly asleep and awoke only when it was night once more.

❀❀❀

"Rome's citizens already spend too much time loafing in hot water," the guest said.

I cannot remember how many desserts there were. The grandest was a vast ship at sea, made of pastry, sugar and almonds and carrying all kinds of fruit.

A·CATASTROPHE

DAY XXIX OF SEPTEMBER

Our small quiet world was turned upside down yesterday. My master seemed weak and ill when he rose in the morning. When he complained of pains in his chest and numbness in his left arm, my mistress tried gently to persuade him not to attend Senate. But he was determined to go and set off in a litter, clutching his vial of sea-grape wine.

We learned later that at the Senate House he had to be almost carried to his favourite seat. The blow came when he stood to speak: his legs would not hold him, and he fell to the ground clutching his chest.

The senators carried him home on a table-top, and here he lies, in a darkened room. His pulse is weak … he speaks few words … he drinks little and eats less.

Outside the silence of his room, my mistress wrings her hands and prays at the shrine by the front door. My master's brother is here. He has used his influence to send a letter to Cratinus by the Emperor's messenger. It travels at the speed of a galloping horse, and will reach him in a day, for he is now stationed not far from Rome. However, even if he hastens back with all possible speed I fear he will be too late.

DAY XXX

During the night a physician came to examine my master. The man was a Greek like me. He arrived with four attendants, but took only my mistress into the bedchamber where my master was lying.

When they came out, he was holding my mistress's hand and reassuring her. However, as they passed a torch-bearer, I glimpsed his eyes clearly and could see from their empty, hopeless look that he did not believe his own words.

An hour later, my master suffered another blow like the one that struck him yesterday. This time he did not recover. Now my master is dead.

My master struck his head on the tiled floor of the Senate House.

52

Even though he was one of the best in Rome, the physician could not help my master.

DAY 1 OF OCTOBER

In the middle of the misery and mourning for my master, I have a reason to be joyful! For the reading of his will has brought a fantastic and wonderful surprise.

Yesterday, my master's brother fetched the will from a temple nearby where it was stored for safe keeping. He took it into the dining room to break the seals, and read the wax panels to the family.

After about half an hour, I heard Cratinus (who arrived yesterday) shouting, then he stormed out of the room in a black mood, followed by everyone else. My master's brother was the last to come out, and he called me over to sit with him in the *peristylum*. There he read to me just as follows (for I borrowed the wax tablets and copied them):

"For her bravery in saving my baby daughter from certain death in the flames of a house-fire, I set free my slave, Iliona, immediately. I also set free her brother Apollo, who shall

be brought from my country estate to be reunited with his sister. In addition I give to Iliona each year the sum of one hundred denarii."

I am free at last!

❀❀❀

"If you had shown your father more respect, he would have shown you more generosity!" my mistress shouted after Cratinus.

53

FREEDOM

DAY III OF NOVEMBER

A month has passed since I last unrolled my diary and sharpened my quills. My life has changed so much – and yet, it seems hardly to have changed at all. Apollo is with me, which makes us both very happy. My mistress sent for him several days after the will was read. He walked all the way to Rome rather than wait for a carriage to fetch him. Now he works here in the house, doing any tasks that require strength and skill – for his months on the farm have given him powerful arms, and hands that learn quickly.

Now that I am free, my mistress treats me better than she did before, and even says "please" and "thank you" if she remembers.

Cytheris did not speak to me for a fortnight. Thankfully, though, we are friends once more.

I am spared some of the tasks I hated most, such as emptying the piss-pots in the morning, but I am still studying, and looking after little Lydia.

Apollo and I have talked about returning to Greece. We could perhaps save enough from our earnings to pay the fare. However, our parents are at the bottom of the sea, and we have few relatives in Mytilini.

Cytheris is still a slave, while I am free.

Furthermore, if pirates were to again attack our ship on the journey, we might swiftly find ourselves back in Rome. Then our story would start again, just as it began a year ago, with chalk on our feet, and wooden signs around our necks.

No, for the present we shall stay here, for my mistress's home is now our home, and her family has become our family too.

Lydia now seems just like a baby sister to me.

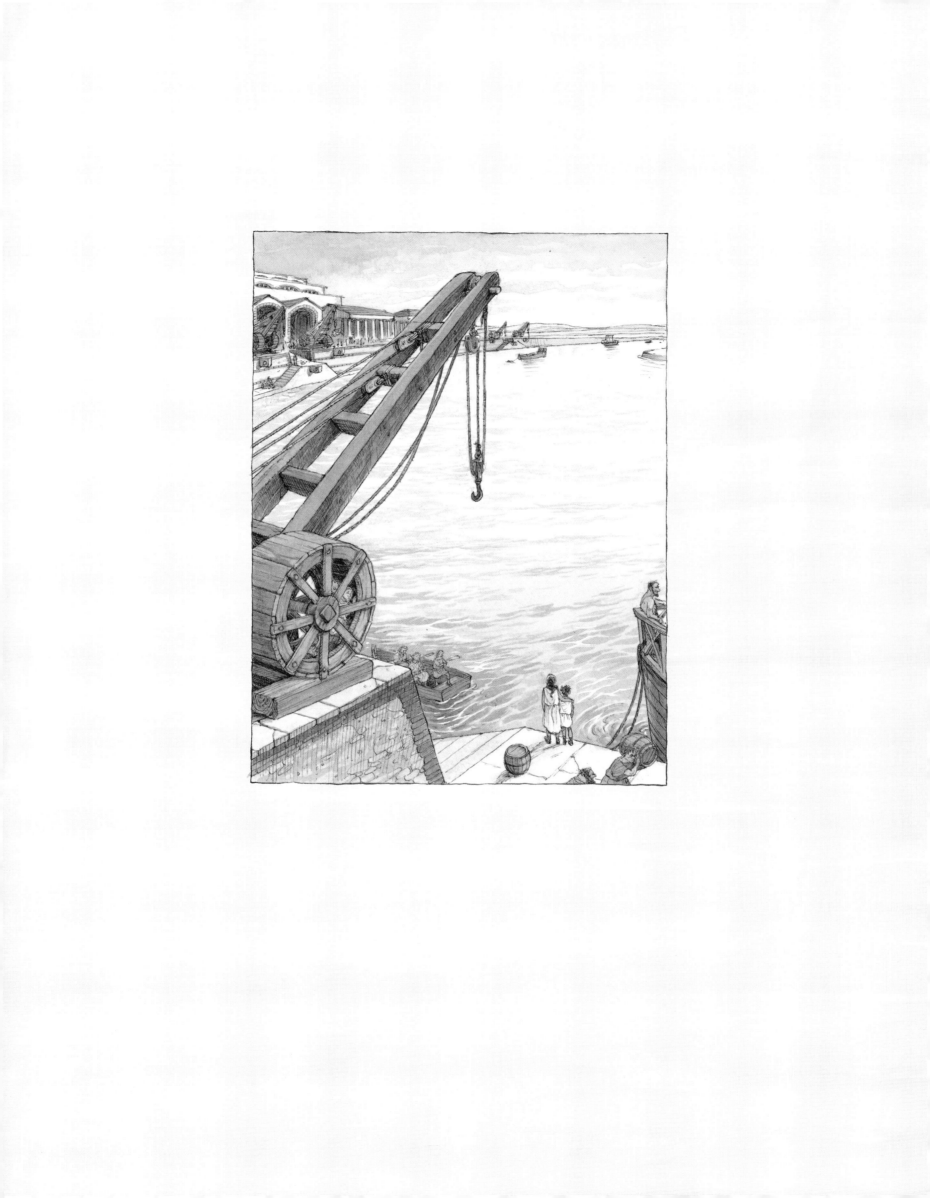

✳ ——— ILIONA'S·WORLD ——— ✳

THOUGH ILIONA'S LIFE IS A STORY, its details are true. Stolen children really did work as slaves in Roman houses. Not all were Greeks: they also came from the many other countries that Rome ruled. For the Romans were the most powerful people in the Ancient World. Over six glorious (and bloodthirsty) centuries they created magnificent art, architecture and writing. Even today we rely on Roman ideas for everything from our laws and calendar to our water supply.

·WHERE WAS ANCIENT ROME?·

Ancient Rome stood where the modern Italian capital city stands today. It was built on seven hills on the banks of the Tiber river.

The Tiber connected Rome to its port, Ostia, where the ship bringing Iliona to the city docked. Beyond Ostia, the lands that the Romans governed stretched from Spain (Hispania) in the west to Syria in the east. Rome ruled Egypt (Aegyptus) in the south, and the northern frontier was England's border with Scotland.

land ruled by the Romans

ROME

·THE CITY·

In AD107 Rome was a busy, thriving centre of trade and industry. Probably three quarters of a million people lived there.

But Rome was an old city even then. People had been living in and farming the Tiber valley for more than 1500 years. According to Roman tradition, the city itself was founded in 753 BC by twin brothers, Romulus and Remus. Romulus gave his name to the city.

·THE EMPIRE·

The Empire was the main source of Rome's great wealth. Each time the Roman armies defeated a hostile nation, they were able to plunder its riches. War booty flowed back to Rome, and with it came huge numbers of prisoners who worked as slaves. Furthermore, the people of the captured regions regularly paid tribute (a kind of tax) to Rome.

WHO WAS WHO?

In the second century AD *emperors* governed Rome. They were not elected, as modern presidents are. They were dictators, and held complete power over the people.

Emperor

Even so, the Roman people liked to believe that they governed themselves and the emperor chose a Senate (parliament) from the city's oldest and most wealthy families. *Senators* advised the emperor, but had real power only in the smaller details of running the city and empire.

Senator

Roman people who were not members of the Senate were called the *citizens* of Rome. Though some were wealthy, citizens also included many poor who owned no land. Even so, they enjoyed some of the same rights and privileges of wealthier Romans.

Citizen

About one twentieth of those who lived in Rome were *freedmen*. These were people who had been born as slaves, but who had won or bought their freedom. Freedmen could become very wealthy, because (unlike some citizens) they could become traders.

Freedman

Slaves were at the bottom of Roman society. They were the property of their masters and could be bought and sold like furniture. The quality of their lives varied tremendously, depending on their owners. Some were beaten and starved like animals. But many lived better than the poorest citizens.

Slaves

·A SLAVE'S LIFE·

Slaves made up between one quarter and one third of the population of ancient Rome, and did all the heaviest, nastiest work.

Wealthy citizens owned astonishing numbers of them: those with farms or factories sometimes had 20,000 or more. They might have bought these labouring slaves at very low prices. However, the best slaves – the intelligent, educated and beautiful – sold for colossal sums.

In early Rome, citizens would put their slaves to death without fear of punishment. However, by the second century, there were laws to protect slaves from the very worst treatment. Some were still beaten, but slaves could at least rely on their own value as protection: only fools destroy their own valuable property.

Slavery made Rome rich, but not all Romans were happy about that: with slaves doing so much of the work, many of Rome's poor – but free – citizens were unemployed, and lived on handouts of free grain and oil.

THE ARMY

It was the Roman soldier who made Rome powerful. Fighting in enormous armies, he conquered all the territory that was to become the Roman Empire. Roman soldiers were well trained, well equipped and not easily frightened. In a battle you'd want them fighting on your side!

·THE STRUCTURE OF THE LEGION·

A small Praetorian Guard protected Rome itself but the main fighting forces were the Roman legions: 30 or so mini-armies trained for conquest abroad.

Legions were made up of 5–6000 foot soldiers (legionnaires), who fought in 80-strong groups called **centuries**, each commanded by a centurion. An officer called the Tribunus Militum commanded **cohorts** of six centuries, and there were ten cohorts in a legion.

·SOLDIERS' EQUIPMENT·

Rome's soldiers did not just fight. They built roads and bridges too. As well as his shield and sword, a soldier carried many other useful things. Altogether his kit weighed about 30 kilos. Soldiers would be expected to march 27 kms a day with this load on their backs, although they had mules to carry the leather tents and the millstones they used to grind their corn into flour.

bronze mess tin

bedding

water kettle

shield

helmet

turf cutter

sword

wooden picket (stake)

javelin

Optio
second in command of the century

a century

Tribunus Militum

Cornicen
horn blower

Signifier
standard bearer

Tesserarius
security chief

Centurion

SPORTS AND GAMES

Just as we do, the Romans loved spectator sports. They were obsessed with the chariot race, supporting one of the four teams – red, green, white and blue. Slaves raced light chariots, drawn by two or four horses, round a vast 600-metre racetrack at breathtaking speeds. It was very dangerous, but a skilled driver became a hero, and could earn enough in prizes to buy his freedom.

Another favourite Roman pastime was the games (*munera*): battles to the death between gladiators (warrior slaves) in a vast, specially-built stadium, the Colosseum. The fights were staged by Rome's wealthiest people to show off their fortunes or to win votes in elections.

Gladiators often killed their opponents, but if the loser in a battle had fought bravely, the cheering crowd could demand that his life be spared. The winners – like chariot drivers – became celebrities.

When simple gladiator fights began to bore the audience, novelties were introduced, such as battles with animals (the fiercer the better) or naval wars in the flooded stadium.

✿✿✿

RELIGION

Roman people prayed to many gods. In early times they had worshipped the spirits of the natural world, and of their dead ancestors. Later, they came to admire Greek religion, and merged their own gods with those of Greece. The Greek god Zeus, for instance, became the Roman god Jupiter.

Rome's priests worshipped all these gods in 100 or so temples in the city, and ordinary Romans joined in festivals each year. But religion could be a private affair too. Every house had a little shrine where people prayed to a small statue of the family spirit. There were similar statues out of doors, particularly at crossroads, where the poor and homeless prayed.

As the Empire grew, so too did interest in cults (the worship of foreign gods). When Christianity spread to Rome it seemed at first like just another cult. However, more and more Romans joined the Christian church and by the end of the fourth century AD, Christianity had become Rome's official religion, replacing all others.

✿✿✿

A charioteer driving a quadriga *– a four-horse chariot.*

TECHNOLOGY

The Romans invented many things that brought lasting practical benefit to large numbers of people. We still use lots of them today.

·CONCRETE·

Long before Roman times, builders bound stones together with mortar, a mixture of lime and water which became hard once it was dry. But Roman engineers mixed mortar with a special kind of sand from the town of Pozzuoli, and so invented concrete. Rammed into wooden moulds, concrete set as hard as rock.

·WATER SUPPLY AND SEWAGE·

As Rome grew, so too did its thirst. Public fountains on every street corner gushed with fresh, clean water. To keep the supply running, engineers built aqueducts across the coutryside to carry channels of water from springs as far as 90 kms away.

This Roman aqueduct could carry two channels of water at the same time.

Rome also had a basic sewage system. Privies (lavatories) and sinks drained into pipes beneath the road outside. These emptied

·ROADS·

To speed the marches of Rome's legions, soldiers built roads as they went. First they surveyed the routes, planning an arrow-straight path across suitable land. Next they dug a pair of trenches to keep the road between them dry and free of mud. The road itself was built in layers like this:

trench for rainwater

stone slabs

large stones

tightly-packed gravel

small stones mixed with cement

in to the *Cloaca Maxima* ("greatest sewer") and then into the River Tiber.

·CENTRAL HEATING·

Thanks to Rome's climate, houses rarely needed heating. Public bath buildings, though, needed to be warmer. They were heated by furnaces built on outside walls. Chimneys drew smoke from the furnace through channels under the floor and behind walls. Called a *hypocaust*, this system was like modern warm-air heating.

·OTHER ROMAN THINGS WE STILL USE:·

- Books with pages are a Roman idea. Previously people wrote on long rolls of paper.
- Many of the laws that govern how we live are based on Roman laws.
- Parliaments with two "houses" follow the pattern of the Roman Republic.
- Romans measured their months by the moon's shape which makes a round ball every 28 days.

- All of us write with the Roman alphabet, though the letters J, U and W were added much later.
- Many of the words that we **use** every day were **originally** in the Latin **language** that the Romans spoke. In these two **sentences** words in bold come from Latin.
- Roman masons arranged half-circles of shaped blocks to hold up wide openings in walls without cement. Arches are still used to build stone bridges and to make grand doorways and light windows.

A Roman arch

- A ring of arches creates a dome: a roof like an upturned bowl. The Romans built the first huge domes and, ever since, architects have used them to keep rooms free of supporting columns.

The dome of the Pantheon in Rome was the largest in the world for over 1700 years.

·A TIMELINE OF ROMAN HISTORY·

The story in this book is of just one year. But the period of Rome's power lasted almost 1500 years. This timeline shows some of the most significant events in that time, so you can get a sense of the empire's history.

BC

753	According to legend, Romulus founds the city of Rome.
509	Romans throw out their evil king and start to govern themselves as a Roman Republic.
264–146	Rome fights Carthage (a rival city in what is now Tunisia) in three Punic Wars. Its victories give it control of most of the Mediterranean, Greece and Syria.
90–82	Civil war breaks out between Rome's noble families and its citizens. A noble – Sulla – wins and rules as a dictator until 79.
73–71	Seventy gladiators, led by the slave Spartacus, escape. 120,000 slaves join them in a revolt.
60	Two politicians, Pompey and Crassus, and a general, Julius Caesar, share power and rule Rome and its empire as a "triumvirate".
53	Crassus dies. Pompey rules while Caesar is away fighting in Gaul (France).
49	Caesar returns to Italy to challenge Pompey.
48	Caesar defeats Pompey at the Battle of Pharsalus.
45	Caesar becomes dictator of Rome.
44	Caesar's rivals murder him. They aim to make Rome a republic again.
43	A consul, Mark Antony, forms a new triumvirate with Caesar's great-nephew, Octavian, and Caesar's ally, Lepidus.
42–32	Octavian and Anthony fight rival politicians, and then each other, for power.
31	Anthony, fighting with Cleopatra, queen of Egypt, is defeated at the battle of Actium.
27	Octavian, Rome's first real "emperor", rules as "Caesar Augustus". He brings peace, good government and wealth to Rome.

AD

2?	Jesus of Nazareth is born in Judea (now Palestine).
14	Caesar Augustus dies and is declared a god.
29?	Jesus is executed on the orders of Judea's Roman governor, Pontius Pilate.
37–41	The cruel Emperor Caligula rules Rome.
41–54	Emperor Claudius rules. He adds Britain to the Roman Empire.
68	The much-hated Emperor Nero kills himself. In the year that follows, four different emperors rule.
79	The volcano Vesuvius erupts in the south of Italy. The towns of Pompeii and Herculaneum are buried for 17 centuries.
98	Trajan becomes emperor. His conquests in Dacia (SE Europe), Nabatia (Jordan) and Parthia (Iran) extend the empire to its maximum size.
115	Jewish people in Egypt, Libya, Cyprus and Judea rebel against Roman rule.
235–284	25 different emperors rule Rome. Chaos engulfs the empire and northern tribes threaten its borders.
285	Emperor Diocletian splits the empire into eastern and western halves to make it easier to govern.
324–337	Emperor Constantine "the Great" reunites the empire and rules from Byzantium (now Istanbul, Turkey). He makes Christianity the official religion.
337	Constantine dies and his sons divide the empire among themselves.
410	German tribes reach the city of Rome and raid it for the first time.
476	The German general Odoacer forces Rome's last emperor out and makes himself king of Italy. The Roman Empire falls.

GLOSSARY·AND·INDEX

Page numbers that are <u>underlined</u> show where unusual words which Romans would have used have already been explained – other unusual words are explained here.

Words shown in *italics* have their own entries, with more information or pages to look up.

A

ABODE 29 Home.
ACTOR 33, 46
ADRANOS <u>36</u>
AEGEAN SEA 5
AFRICA, AFRICAN 38, 49
AGRIPPA'S BATHS 36 The first baths in Rome, built by Emperor Agrippa. See also *baths, Nero's baths.*
ALEXANDRIA 5 An important city in *Egypt.*
ALPHABET 61 See also *letters.*
AMPHITHEATRE 40, 44
AMPHORA 28 A vase for carrying and storing *water* or *oil.*
ANCESTORS 59 Family members who died a long time in the past.
ANIMALS 41, 57, 59 See also *dogs, horses.*
APARTMENTS 18–19
AQUEDUCT <u>14</u>, 28–29, 60
ARCHES 61
ARCHITECT, ARCHITECTURE 45, 56, 61
ARMOUR 20, 22, 40
ASIA MINOR 38 A Roman *province* situated roughly where Turkey is today.
ASSES 18 Coins of small value.
ATRIUM 20, 21 An open courtyard in the centre of a Roman home.
AUCTION 8–9

AUGUSTUS 36, 38 The *Latin* name for August.

B

BAILIFF <u>32</u>–33 See also *overseer.*
BANQUET 48–51
BARGE 8
BATHS 14–17, 36, 44, 46, 49, 60 See also *Agrippa's baths, Nero's baths.*
BEARERS 23
BETS 26, 43
BOOKS 60
BRIDGE 28–29, 61
BRITANNIA 38 Roman Britain, including England and Wales but not Scotland.

C

CALDARIUM 14
CALENDAR 12, 56
CASTELLUM 29 The part of an *aqueduct* designed to store *water.*
CENTURIES <u>58</u>
CENTURION <u>58</u>
CHARIOT 23, 59
CHRISTIANITY 59, 61 The religion based on the teachings of Jesus Christ.
CITIZEN 12, 29, 43, 57, 61
COHORTS <u>58</u>
COLOSSEUM 59
CONCRETE 60
CRESCENT 26 A curved shape resembling the moon.
CULT <u>59</u>

D

DACIA, DACIAN 18, 21, 38, 40, 61 A large area of south-eastern Europe, roughly where Romania is today. It was conquered by *Trajan*

in 106 AD and became a *province* of the *Roman Empire.*
DECEBALUS 21 The general who led the *Dacian* army in resisting the Romans.
DECK RAIL 7
DENARIUS 18, 39, 53 A coin, worth about ten *asses.*
DICE 22
DICTATOR 57, 61 An unelected ruler.
DIGNITARIES 22 People with important positions in society.
DOGS 18, 33, 35, 36
DOME <u>61</u>
DOMUS 9 Home.
DONKEYS 8, 30 See also *mules.*

E

EGYPT, EGYPTIAN 5, 6, 38, 56, 61
EMPEROR 18, 20–24, 40–41, 44, 45, 57, 61
ENTERTAINERS 49
ESTATE 26, 53 A collection of land, houses and farms belonging to a wealthy *citizen.*

F

FIG 19, 20
FIRE 36–37, 53
FLOATS 22–23
FOOD 48–51
FORUM 23, 26, 38
FOUNTAIN 28–29, 60
FREEDMEN <u>57</u>
FREEDOM 12, 15, 19, 41, 57, 59
FRIGIDARIUM 14
FUGITIVUS <u>35</u>, 36

G

GALLEY 5 A long, low ship with sails and oars.

GAMES 40, <u>59</u> See also *munera*.

GAUL 38 A *province* of the *Roman Empire*, situated where France is today.

GLADIATOR 40–41, 59

GODS 23, 59, 61

GOSSIP 36

GREEK 5, 8, 9, 11, 18–19, 22, 29, 33, 34, 44–45, 52, 56, 59

H

HANDOUTS <u>57</u>

HECKLE 46 To shout abuse.

HORSES 23, 31, 59

HYPOCAUST <u>60</u>

I

ITALY 56, 61

IUNIUS 18, 20, 22, 26 The *Latin* name for June.

IULIUS 28, 30, 32, 34 The *Latin* name for July.

J

JAVELIN 58 A long, light spear used as a weapon.

JULIUS CAESAR 61 A powerful politician, general and, later, *dictator*.

JUPITER 59

JUPITER (TONANS) <u>30</u>

L

LABOURERS 34 Farm workers.

LATIN 8–9, 11, 15, 19, 33, 46, 61 The language of Rome.

LAUREL WREATH 23

LAWS 26, 56, 60

LEGION <u>58</u>, 60

LEGIONNAIRE 18, 58

LETTERS 6, 34 The *alphabet*.

LIME 45, 60 A white powder produced by burning limestone.

LITTER 14, 52 Seat mounted on two poles, upon which a master could be carried around by his *slaves*. See also *sedan chair*.

LOT 9 Goods sold together at *auction*.

M

MAIUS 12, 14, 18 The *Latin* name for May.

MAMILLARES 14 Cloth to tie around the chest.

MAMME <u>29</u>

MANUMISSION <u>15</u>, 18

MARBLE 20, 27, 39, 44

MARINER 6 A sailor.

MASON 44–45, 61 See also *stonemasons*.

MORTAR 60

MULES 30, 58 See also *donkeys*.

MUNERA <u>40</u>, 59 See also *games*.

MYTILINI 5, 13, 15, 20, 30, 33, 47, 54

N

NAVAL WARS 59

NERO'S BATHS 14, 44, 46 See also *Agrippa's baths*, *baths*.

NET-MAN <u>40</u>–43

NICHE 26 A space set into the wall where small objects are kept.

O

OFFERING 30 A gift to the *gods*.

OIL 8, 14, 15, 38

OLIVES 8, 31, 34, 35

OMEN 30 Something people believe gives a clue to what will happen in the future.

ORNATRIX 39 A hairdresser.

OSTIA 8, 56

OVERSEER 4, 9–11, 15, 35 Someone who supervised workers on behalf of their master. See also *bailiff*.

OX 13

P

PACE 19 A distance equivalent to the length of a stride.

PANTOMIME <u>46</u>

PAPYRUS 5, 6

PEDAGOGUS 12 A tutor.

PERISTYLUM 20, 36, 53 A covered courtyard surrounding a small garden.

PHYSICIAN 52–53 A doctor.

PIRATE 6–7, 54

PLUNDER 57 To steal, usually using force.

POMPEY 46, 61 A military leader and ally of *Julius Caesar*.

POSTMAN 31

POZZOLANA 45

PRAETORIAN GUARD 58

PRIEST 30, 59

PRIVIES <u>60</u>

PROVINCES 38 The lands that were part of the *Roman Empire*.

PURSUER 40–43

Q

QUADRANS <u>14</u>, 19

QUILLS 5, 54 A pen made from a feather, sharpened at its tip.

R

RAEDA 30, 31 A covered wagon.

SOURCES

Writers and illustrators owe a debt of gratitude to the authors and artists whose works inspire them. Richard Platt and David Parkins are especially grateful because they searched in more than seventy books for details that would make the text and pictures of Roman Diary authentic. There isn't room here to list them all, but the following are among the more recently published books.

Adkins, Lesley & Roy: A Dictionary of Roman Religion

Beacham, Richard C.: Spectacle Entertainments of Early Imperial Rome

Bennett, Julian: Trajan, Optimus Princeps

Biesty, Stephen: Rome in Spectacular Cross-section

Bradley, Keith: Slavery and Society at Rome

Carcopino, Jérôme: Daily Life in Ancient Rome

Connolly, Peter: The Ancient City

Casson, Lionel: Everyday Life in Ancient Rome

James, Simon: Ancient Rome

Langley, Andrew and de Souza, Philip: Roman News

Marks, Anthony and Tingay, Graham: The Romans

Paoli, Ugo Enrico: Rome, its People, Life and Customs

Richardson, Lawrence: A New Topographical Dictionary of Ancient Rome

Robinson, O. F.: Ancient Rome, City Planning and Administration